BAXTER BARRET BROWN'S BASS FIDDLE

04-15-05

All my best wishes to you!

BY TIM A. McKENZIE ♫ ILLUSTRATIONS BY CHARLES SHAW

This is Baxter Barret Brown.

And this is
Baxter
Barret,
Brown's Bass Fiddle.

Baxter loved to play the Bass Fiddle. He loved the big, low sounds it made,

and he played it all day long.

Then one day Baxter decided he wanted to take his Bass Fiddle with him wherever he went.

So he got his bicycle, his hammer, and his wrench;

and when he was finished hammering
and wrenching,
he had mounted the wheels
on the bottom and the handlebars
on the top with the seat.

He put a great big
"AH·OOO·GAH" horn on
the front and
called it

BAXTER BARRET BROWN'S
BASS FIDDLE BICYCLE.

Then off down the road he went.

Soon, BAXTER came upon a lake. There were all kinds

of boats floating on the lake, and BAXTER decided he wanted one, too.

So...

he put a rudder and an anchor on the back, a ship's wheel on top with his handlebars; and a sail behind his seat. He called it BAXTER BARRE

BROWN'S BASS FIDDLE BICYCLE BOAT,

and off to the water he went.

As BAXTER was enjoying the ride on his new BASS FIDDLE BOAT, he looked around the lake and saw all of the nice beach front homes on the shoreline.

He decided he wanted one, too. So...

he set his BASS FIDDLE BICYCLE BOAT up on the beach and cut a door into the side.

Then he got a bed,

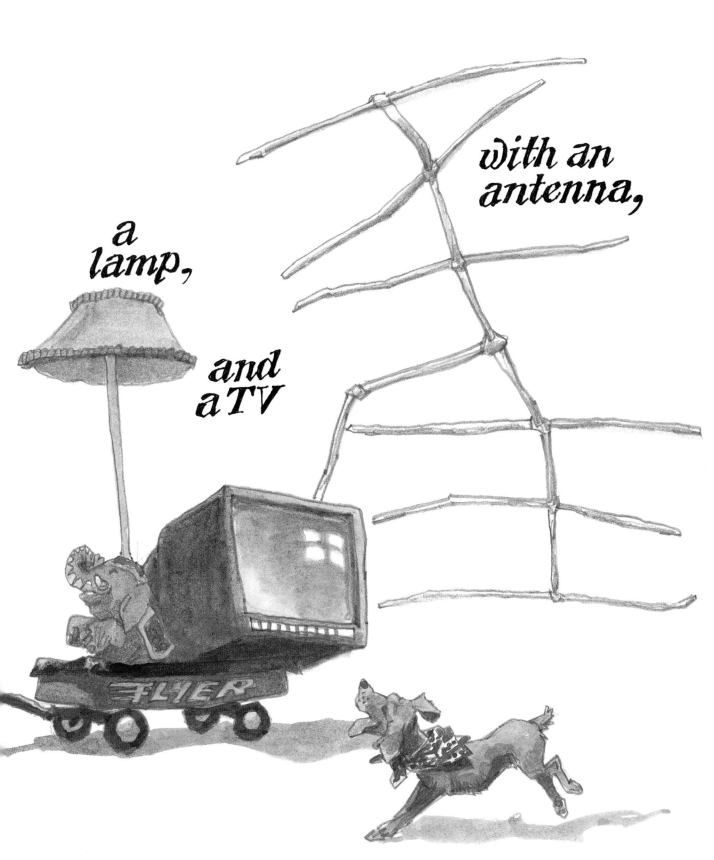

a
lamp,

and
a TV

with an
antenna,

and a potbellied stove with a pipe chimney.

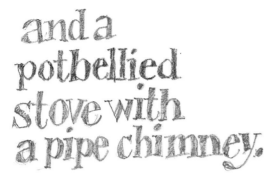

Then he built a boat dock so he could do some fishing, and he called it

BAXTER BARRET BROWN'S
BASS FIDDLE BICYCLE
BOAT BEACH FRONT
BUNGALOW.

As BAXTER was relaxing and
enjoying his new BEACH FRONT BUNGALOW,
he decided this was a good time for
a bass fiddle song. So...

He climbed upon his
BASS FIDDLE BICYCLE
BOAT BEACH FRONT
BUNGALOW to play,
but BAXTER
couldn't play at all.

The handlebars
and the ship's wheel
and the sails and the
wheels and the big
"AH-OOO-GAH" horn
and the bicycle seat
and the stove pipe
chimney and the
rudder and the
TV antenna were
all in the way.

BAXTER was very sad.

He couldn't do what really made him happy any more.

He realized he had traded something he really loved for a lot of things he didn't need.

BAXTER decided to undo everything.

First he threw out
the bed,
the TV,
and lamp,
and the
potbellied stove.

Then he took off the
TV antenna,
and the sails,
and the rudder,
and the handlebars,
and the ship's wheel

AND SO

ON AND SO ON UNTIL....

all that was left was the
big **BASS FIDDLE** and lots
of room to play it.

BAXTER loved having his big BASS FIDDLE back the way it was.

But then...

an airplane
flew by . . . .

bright sky press
Box 416
Albany, Texas 76430

10 9 8 7 6 5 4 3 2 1

Library of Congress Cataloging-in-Publication Data

McKenzie, Tim A., 1956–
    Baxter Barret Brown's bass fiddle / by Tim A. McKenzie ; drawings by Charles Shaw.
        p. cm.
    Summary: Baxter Barret Brown loves playing his bass fiddle so much that he wants to
take it with him everywhere, so he attaches wheels and other gadgets, adding more and
more until he discovers that he can no longer play—and that is what he wants to do most of all.
    ISBN 1-931721-06-8 (alk. paper)
    [1. Musicians–Fiction. 2. Violoncello–Fiction. 3. Humorous stories.] I. Shaw, Charles,
1941– ill. II. Title.

PZ7.M4786762Bax2004
[E]-dc22

2003069630

Cover design by Isabel Lasater Hernandez

Printed in Hong Kong through Asia Pacific Offset